PJ MASKS

Into the Night to Save the Day!

Based on the episode "Catboy vs. Robo-Cat"

Simon Spotlight
New York London Toronto Sydney New Delhi

SIMON SPOTLIGHT
An imprint of Simon & Schuster Children's Publishing Division
1230 Avenue of the Americas, New York, New York 10020
This Simon Spotlight paperback edition January 2017

Adapted by Cala Spinner from the series PJ Masks

For information about special discounts for bulk purchases, please contact Simon & Schuster Special Sales at 1-866-506-1949 or business@simonandschuster.com.
Manufactured in the United States of America 0118 LAK
10 9 8 7 6 5
ISBN 978-1-4814-8645-3 (pbk)
ISBN 978-1-4814-8646-0 (eBook)

Connor, Greg, and Amaya are playing outside with their flying discs. "Kicking Cartwheel!" Amaya cheers as she catches the disc.

"Swirling Spin!" Greg shouts, catching another. Greg throws his disc to Connor, but it soars into the garden instead. Connor runs after it.

When Connor returns, his friends are gone! Their two flying discs are on the ground, and there's a circuit board underneath them. What could a circuit board be doing there?

“This is a mission for the PJ Masks!” Connor says. “Well, one of us, anyway. *This* PJ Mask is on his way . . . into the night to save the day!”

Connor becomes Catboy!

Catboy analyzes the circuit board with the PJ Picture Player. The circuit board is from a robot, and a robot means Romeo is behind this!

Catboy speeds through the city in his Cat-Car to track down Romeo.

“Romeo!” Catboy shouts when he finds the troublemaker. “What have you done with my friends?”

“They're here,” Romeo sneers, “but they work for me now!”

“We will only obey Romeo,” Owlette says.

Just then Catboy hears a noise overhead.

Catboy looks up—Greg and Amaya are trapped in cages! Amaya explains that Romeo captured them when they were playing outside.

"But if you're in those cages, who are they?" asks Catboy, pointing toward Gekko and Owlette.

That's when Catboy realizes—they aren't Gekko and Owlette. They're robots!

“If I hadn’t lost my circuit board, you would have been a robot too!” Romeo says.

“You mean this?” says Catboy. He holds up the circuit board he found.

Romeo’s eyes widen. “Soon my Robo-Owl and Robo-Gekko will put you in a cage too!”

“Catboy, free us so we can help you!” Amaya calls from her cage.

“Not without your powers!” Catboy shouts back. “But don’t worry. I’ll get your pajamas back from Romeo!”

Catboy leaps into the Cat-Car to get away from the robots, but he lands upside down. Robo-Gekko jumps into the passenger seat beside him and pushes the eject button.

Catboy's seat flies out of the car, and the robots drive the Cat-Car back to Romeo!

"Look!" Greg shouts as he watches the robots pull up. "They took Catboy's Cat-Car!"

"I *know* we can help Catboy, even without our powers . . . ," Amaya says sadly.

Greg has an idea! "Let's take this cage apart. Give me your hairpin so I can unscrew this bar."

Catboy arrives on the scene, climbing onto the cages. "Stop trying to escape," he whispers to his friends. "Without your powers you'll be safer up here."

But then Catboy loses his balance and falls. Romeo sees what they're up to and sends in his robots!

"At least I still have this," Catboy says, pulling out the circuit board. But Robo-Gekko swipes it right out of his hand!

"Now that I have the missing piece, I can activate my Robo-Cat! Mwahahaha!" Romeo laughs.

He slides open a door in his lab and reveals—Robo-Cat!

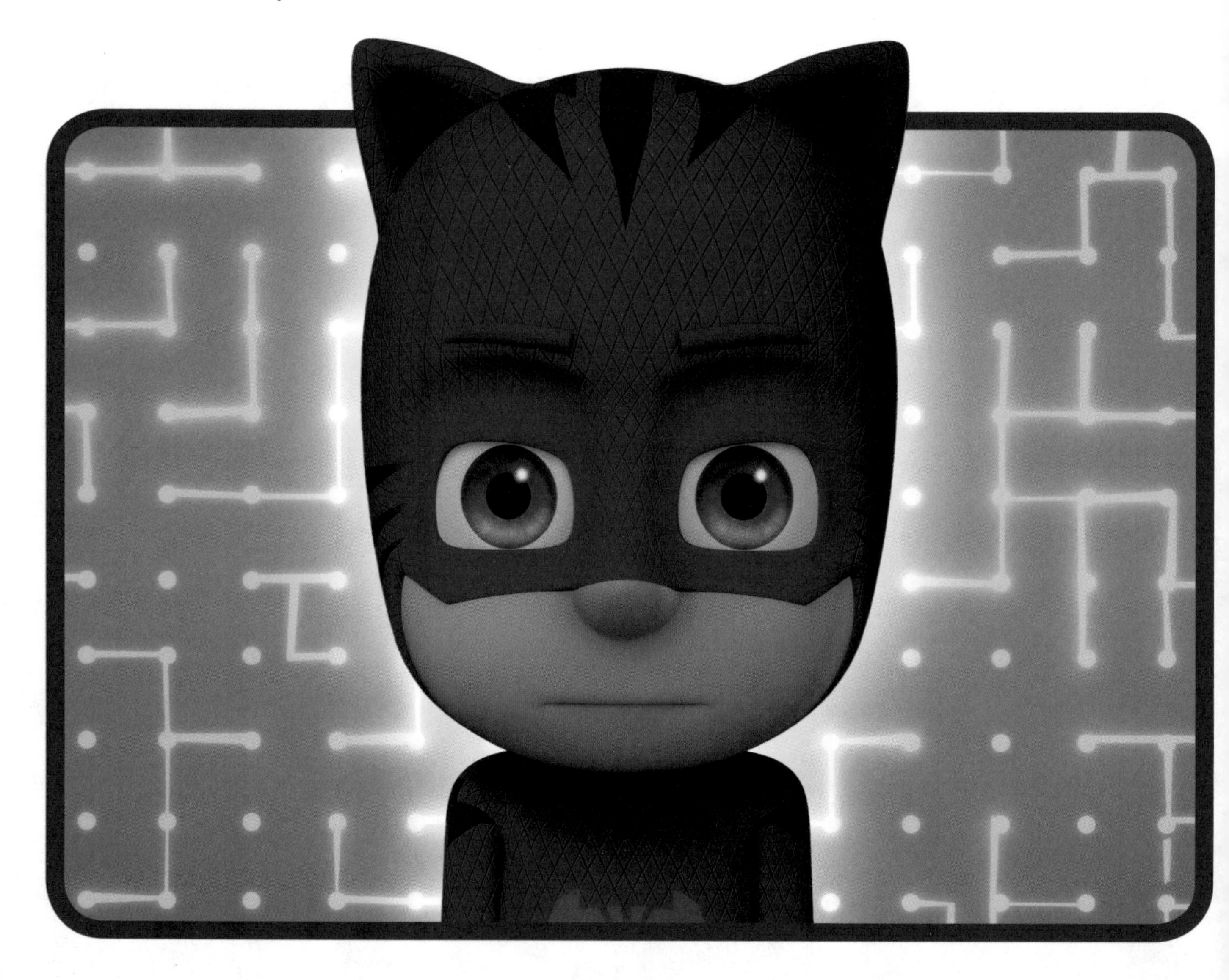

Catboy has a plan. He needs to take back Greg's and Amaya's pajamas so they can become Gekko and Owlette, but Romeo has other ideas.

"Robo-Cat, lock that pussycat up," Romeo commands.

Just then a flying disc appears! It knocks Robo-Cat off his feet.
"Greg and Amaya to the rescue!" Amaya shouts.
Catboy looks behind him and sees . . . Greg and Amaya, standing free!

Catboy smiles. "You guys really are amazing—even without your powers. You were right. I *should* have let you help out."

Before Greg and Amaya can respond, Romeo commands Robo-Gekko and Robo-Owl to catch the heroes.

“It’s time to be a hero and let you guys help,” Catboy tells his friends. “Super Cat Speed!” He zips past the robots, grabs the pajamas, and gives them to his friends.

Gleefully, Greg and Amaya put their pajamas on.

Greg becomes Gekko!

Amaya becomes Owlette!

"We need to get to Romeo's supercomputer to stop the robots," Owlette says.

But before Owlette can say anything else, the robots tackle her and Gekko. Catboy can't tell his friends apart from the robots!

"Now what, kitty-litter boy? You can't tell them apart!" Romeo says, delighted.

"Your robots may have superpowers, but they're not *friends* like we are!" Catboy says. He flings two metal lids into the air, just like flying discs!

"Kicking Cartwheel!" the real Owlette shouts.

"Swirling Spin!" the real Gekko cheers.

"See, Romeo? I know who my friends are. Ready for our special move?" Catboy says.

He flings his metal lid at the rope that holds up Amaya's and Greg's cages. The cages fall and trap Robo-Gekko!

Owlette and Gekko throw their lids and knock out Robo-Owl and Robo-Cat!

Then Catboy throws another lid directly at Romeo's supercomputer. . . .

BAM! The robots power down, this time for good.

"No! My supercomputer!" Romeo cries. "You'll pay for this next time, PJ Masks!"

The PJ Masks watch as Romeo takes off in his lab.

"Looks like Romeo won't be back for a while, now that his supercomputer has been destroyed," Catboy says happily. "With or without our superpowers, we're an amazing team."

PJ Masks all shout hooray! 'Cause in the night, we saved the day!